For Bradford, a man's best friend
come rain or shine
– O. H.

For my bestest friends Mike and Karen,
always there to fix my leaky windows
– C. P.

tiger tales

5 River Road, Suite 128, Wilton, CT 06897

Published in the United States 2021

Text by Owen Hart

Text copyright © 2021 Little Tiger Press Ltd.

Illustrations copyright © 2021 Caroline Pedler

ISBN-13: 978-1-68010-249-9

ISBN-10: 1-69010-249-4

Printed in China

LTP/2800/3491/1020

2 4 6 8 10 9 7 5 3 1

www.tigertalesbooks.com

The Forest Stewardship Council® (FSC®) is an international, non-governmental organization dedicated to promoting responsible management of the world's forests. FSC® operates a system of forest certification and product labeling that allows consumers to identify wood and wood-based products from well-managed forests.

For more information about the FSC®, please visit their website at www.fsc.org

The Bear in the Boat

by Owen Hart

Illustrated by
Caroline Pedler

tiger tales

The rain just wouldn't stop falling.
Puddles were everywhere.
But Bear didn't mind.

She had a plan for everything.

"Good morning, Squirrel," she called through the raindrops. "Here's a basket of food if you get hungry. I heard that the food you collected was ruined by the rain."

"How kind!" chattered Squirrel.
"I hope I'll be safe in my tree.
You certainly will be, high up
on your hill!"

Bear smiled. "Let's hope we'll
all be safe," she said.

Bear's next stop was Hedgehog's house.

"This puddle creeps closer every time I turn my back," he fretted.

"Then let's send it someplace else," said Bear.

With her paw, she dug a path for the water to follow.

Bear had plans for Mouse and Rabbit, too.

"This log will make a barricade," she declared. "No one wants a soggy burrow."

"Yes!" agreed Rabbit. "My paws are getting soaked!"

"Thank you!" said Mouse.
At last, Bear's work was done.

Safe at home, Bear hummed to the song of the rain.

Dripping and dropping.

Tickling and trickling.

Just then . . .

Knock!
Knock!

"Our barricade was swept away!"
grumped Rabbit.
"Ooo! You should have seen it!"
Mouse added, her whiskers twitching.

Bear knew what to do.
"Don't worry! Come inside!" she told them.

There were cushions and blankets for everyone.

"Bear has a plan for everything!" said Mouse.

Soon, they heard a voice calling —

"Help! Help! Are you there?"

It was Hedgehog.

"The puddle came back. And
it's bigger than EVER!" he cried.

"Bear! Your doormat!"
squeaked Mouse as the
water carried it away.

"The river has overflowed its
banks!" gasped Rabbit.

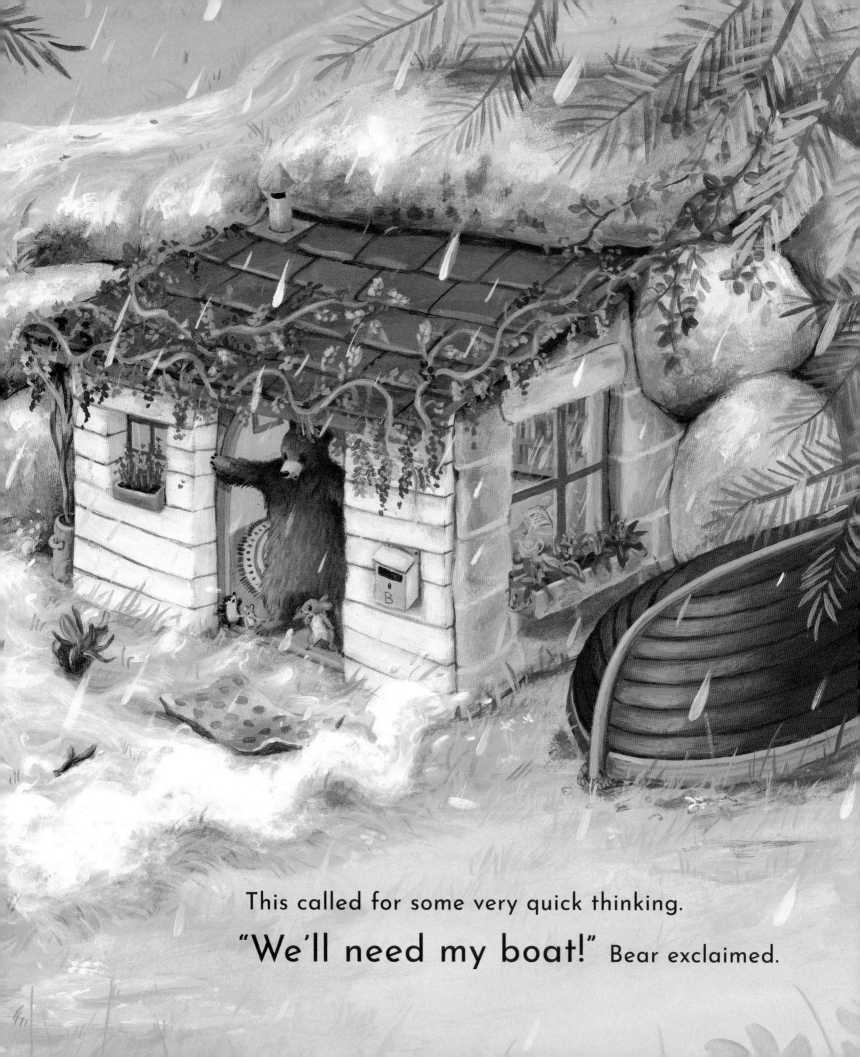

This called for some very quick thinking.
"We'll need my boat!" Bear exclaimed.

Bear's boat was sturdy and big enough for all of them. Bear reached down to turn it over.

But even with a bear's strength, the boat would not budge.

Poor Bear. First her home, and now her boat!

"All my planning!" she groaned. "And now we'll be washed away!"

"Not with friends by your side,"
said Hedgehog, rushing to help.
Even Rabbit pushed and pushed
as the water inched closer.

Then the boat began to move. "There we go!" puffed Bear.
And with one last push. . .

. . . the friends set sail!

At first, the animals were a cheerful crew.
They hummed a tune. They took turns rowing.
But all around was water and treetops, with
no land in sight.

"Where will we go?" said Mouse at last.
"And what will we EAT?" asked Rabbit.
This time, Bear had no plan.

But then came a voice they all knew . . . .

"Hellooo! Is anyone there?"

It was Squirrel floating toward them.

"I was swept right out of my tree!" he chattered.

"But now you're safe!" cheered Bear. "And there's food for all of us!"

The friends shared the food.

"Things always feel so much better with friends by your side," said Bear.

They drifted along, sharing stories, until at last . . . *BUMP!*

"Land ho!" called Mouse,
hopping out of the boat.
"And the rain!" gasped Rabbit.
"It stopped!"

Even though their adventure
was over, their friendship would
last forever.